THE BIGGEST JOB OF ALL

Harriet Ziefert

Pictures by Lauren Browne

For Alison
—H.Z.

For Elise
—L.B.

Published in the United States 2005 by
Blue Apple Books
515 Valley Street, Maplewood, N.J. 07040
www.blueapplebooks.com
Distributed in the U.S. by Chronicle Books

First Edition
Printed in China
ISBN: 1-59354-100-7
1 3 5 7 9 10 8 6 4 2
1424645

"Mommy, when I am
all grown up,
I want to have a
really big job."

"Maybe you'll take care
of a baby, Lulu."

"No, Mommy, that's not what I mean."

"Maybe you'll invite lots of people
and make a big party."

"No, Mommy,
that's not what I mean."

"Mommy, I mean a really, really big job."

"Well, Lulu dear, maybe you'll wash an elephant."

"Mommy, you're being silly!
I don't want to wash an elephant. I'll get all wet."

"Lulu, you could be a teacher.
That's a big and important job."

"I don't want to be a teacher.
Teachers have to wipe noses, tie shoelaces,
and fix stuck zippers."

"Would you rather be a doctor
or a nurse, Lulu?"

"No, Mommy.
I don't like medicine and
I don't like shots."

"Lulu, you could drive a big rig,
or operate a big crane."

"Mommy, I don't
want to wear a hard hat.
Hats itch."

"Mommy, what's a really,
really big job—

the biggest job you know?"

"Actually, Lulu, the biggest job I know
is taking care of your brother and you.
It's the most important job I know."

"Mommy, are you sure?"

"I'm sure, Lulu.
It's a really big and
really important job."

"Then I'd like to be a mommy—
a mommy just like you.
I love you, Mommy."

"Lulu, I love you too. Good night.
And may all your dreams come true."

"Mommy . . .

. . . could I also be an author,
just like you?"

"Maybe you will
do that too, Lulu.
But now it's time
to close your eyes
and to start dreaming."

"Good night, Lulu."